# WRITTEN BY JON SCIESZKA

CHARACTERS AND ENVIRONMENTS DEVELOPED BY THE

**DAVID SHANNON**   **LOREN LONG**   **DAVID GORDON**

ILLUSTRATION CREW:

Executive producer: TOR INDUSTRIES in association with Animagic S.L.

Creative supervisor: Nina Rappaport Brown ○ Drawings by: Juan Pablo Navas ○ Color by: Antonio Reyna

Color assistant: Gabriela Lazbal ○ Art director: Karin Paprocki

## READY-TO-ROLL

ALADDIN

NEW YORK   LONDON   TORONTO   SYDNEY

ALADDIN

An imprint of Simon & Schuster

Children's Publishing Division

1230 Avenue of the Americas, New York, NY 10020

First Aladdin paperback edition February 2010

Text and illustrations copyright © 2010 by JRS Worldwide, LLC.

ALADDIN is a trademark of Simon & Schuster, Inc.,

and related logo is a registered trademark of Simon & Schuster, Inc.

READY-TO-READ is a registered trademark of Simon & Schuster, Inc.

TRUCKTOWN and JON SCIESZKA'S TRUCKTOWN and design

are trademarks of JRS Worldwide, LLC.

For information about special discounts for bulk purchases,

please contact Simon & Schuster Special Sales at 1-866-506-1949

or business@simonandschuster.com.

The Simon & Schuster Speakers Bureau can bring authors

to your live event. For more information or to book an event

contact the Simon & Schuster Speakers Bureau at 1-866-248-3049

or visit our website at www.simonspeakers.com.

The text of this book was set in Truck King.

Manufactured in the United States of America

10 9 8 7 6 5 4 3 2 1

Library of Congress Cataloging-in-Publication Data

Scieszka, Jon.

Melvin's valentine / written by Jon Scieszka ;

characters and environments developed by Design Garage ;

drawings by Juan Pablo Navas ; color by Isabel Nadal. — First Aladdin ed.

p. cm.

Summary: Melvin the cement mixer worries when he cannot figure out who gave him a valentine.

[1. Trucks—Fiction. 2. Worry—Fiction. 3. Valentines—Fiction.] I. Title. / PZ7.S41267 Mh 2010

[E]—dc22 / 2008030723

ISBN 978-1-4169-4144-6 (pbk) / ISBN 978-1-4169-4155-2 (lib)

Melvin got  a valentine.

But he did not know
who it was from.

This made Melvin worry.

This made Melvin
worry more.

"Beep, beep."
Rita laughed.

"Nope," said Jack.

This made Melvin worry
even more.

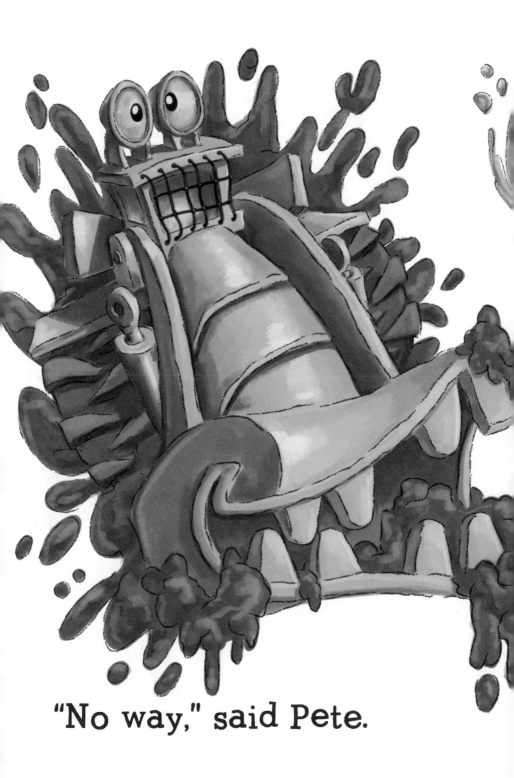

"No way," said Pete.

Melvin was really
worried.

"Beep, beep," Rita called.

"Hey, Melvin," said Rita.
"I am so glad you showed
everyone my valentine."

"YOUR valentine?"
said Melvin.